THIS BOOK IS DEDICATED
TO MY CHILDREN.
MIRRELLE, MICHAEL, MARIANNA, MADDIX,
MYLES, AND PHEONIX.

MY ADVICE:
NO MATTER HOW OLD YOU ARE, CHASE YOUR DREAMS
WITH THE WONDER OF A WIDE EYED CHILD.

Red Rudy, Red Rudy,
Lost his booty.
Where o' where
could it be?

HE LOOKED IN,
HE LOOKED OUT.

HE LOOKED AROUND ABOUT.

HE LOOKED AS FAR

THE EYE COULD SEE.

He looked up,
He looked down,
in the lake,
at the mound.

UNDER THE CAR,
UNDER THE TOOLS,
IN THE MEADOW,
IN THE POOL.

HE WISHED IT
WOULD MAKE A SOUND.

He looked by the water, and on land.

He looked in the air,
and dug in the sand.

He looked at the hotel,
and with the band.
He cradled his head,
in his hands.

Think, think Red Rudy, Where did you go?

Now he remembers!
Its hidden at the chateau!

www.ingramcontent.com/pod-product-compliance
Lightning Source LLC
Chambersburg PA
CBHW041545240626
47164CB00002B/130